little Miss Naughty

by Roger Hargreaves

WORLD INTERNATIONAL
MANCHESTER

Are you ever naughty?

Sometimes, I bet!

Well, little Miss Naughty was naughty all the time.

She awoke one Sunday morning and looked out of the window.

"Looks like a nice day," she thought to herself.

And then she grinned.

"Looks like a nice day for being naughty," she said.

And rubbed her hands!

That Sunday Mr Uppity was out for his morning stroll.

Little Miss Naughty knocked his hat off his head.

And jumped on it!

"My hat!" cried Mr Uppity.

That afternoon Mr Clever was sitting in his garden reading a book.

And do you know what that little Miss Naughty did?

She broke his glasses!

"My glasses!" cried Mr Clever.

That evening Mr Bump was just standing there.

Minding his own business.

And guess what little Miss Naughty did?

She ran off with his bandages!

And bandaged up Mr Small!

"Mmmmmmmmmmfffffff!" he cried.

It's difficult to say anything when you're bandaged up like that!

Mr Uppity and Mr Clever and Mr Bump and Mr Small were very very very very cross.

Very very very very cross indeed!

"Oh what a wonderful Sunday," giggled little Miss Naughty as she walked along.

"And it isn't even bedtime yet!"

First thing on Monday morning the Mr Men had a meeting.

"Something has to be done," announced Mr Uppity, who had managed to straighten out his hat.

They all looked at Mr Clever, who was wearing his spare pair of glasses.

"You're the cleverest," they said. "What's to be done about little Miss Naughty?"

Mr Clever thought.

He cleared his throat.

And spoke.

"I've no idea," he said.

"I have," piped up Mr Small.

"I know what that naughty little lady needs," he went on.

"And I know who can do it," he added.

"What?" asked Mr Uppity.

"Who?" asked Mr Clever.

"Aha!" chuckled Mr Small, and went off to see a friend of his.

Somebody who could do impossible things.

Somebody who could do impossible things like making himself invisible.

I wonder who that could be?

That Monday Mr Nosey was asleep under a tree.

Little Miss Naughty crept towards him with a pot of paint in one hand, a paintbrush in the other, and a rather large grin on her face.

She was going to paint the end of his nose!

Red!

But.

Just as she was about to do the dreadful deed,
something happened.

TWEAK!

Somebody tweaked her nose!

Somebody she couldn't see tweaked her nose!

Somebody invisible!

I wonder who?

"Ouch!" cried little Miss Naughty.

And, dropping the paint and paintbrush,
she ran away as fast as her little legs would
carry her.

On Tuesday Mr Busy was rushing along.

As usual!

Little Miss Naughty, standing by the side of the road, stuck out her foot.

She was going to trip him up!

Head over heels!

And heels over head!

But.

Just before she did, something happened.

TWEAK!

The invisible nose tweaker had struck again!

And it hurt!

"Ouch!" cried little Miss Naughty.

And ran away even faster than her little legs would carry her.

On Wednesday Mr Happy was at home.

Watching television!

Outside, little Miss Naughty picked up a stone.

She was going to break his window!

Naughty girl!

But.

As she brought her arm back to throw, guess what?

That's right!

TWEAK!

"Ouch!" cried little Miss Naughty as she ran off holding her nose.

And so it went on.

All day Thursday.

TWEAK!

All day Friday.

TWEAK! TWEAK!

All day Saturday.

TWEAK! TWEAK! TWEAK!

By which time little Miss Naughty's nose was bright red.

But.

By Sunday she was cured.

No naughtiness at all!

Thanks to the invisible nose tweaker.

On Sunday evening Mr Small went round to see him.

"Hello Mr Impossible," he smiled.

"Thank you for helping to cure little Miss Naughty."

"My pleasure," laughed Mr Impossible.

"But it did take all week."

Mr Small grinned.

"Don't you mean," he said. "All tweak?"

MORE SPECIAL OFFERS
FOR MR MEN AND LITTLE MISS READERS

In every Mr Men and Little Miss book like this one, <u>and now</u> in the Mr Men sticker and activity books, you will find a special token. Collect six tokens and we will send you a gift of your choice.

Choose either a <u>Mr Men</u> or <u>Little Miss</u> poster, <u>or</u> a Mr Men or Little Miss **double sided** full colour bedroom door hanger.

Return this page <u>with six tokens per gift required</u> to
arketing Dept., MM / LM Gifts, World International Ltd., Deanway Technology Centre, Wilmslow Road, Handforth, Cheshire SK9 3FB

|— 100 mm —|

our name:_____ Age: _____

ddress: _____

_____

_____Postcode: _____

arent / Guardian Name (Please Print) _____

ase tape a 20p coin to your request to cover part post and package cost

nclose <u>six</u> tokens per gift, please send me:-

sters:-	Mr Men Poster ☐	Little Miss Poster ☐
or Hangers -	Mr Nosey / Muddle ☐	Mr Greedy / Lazy ☐
	Mr Tickle / Grumpy ☐	Mr Slow / Quiet ☐
	Mr Messy / Noisy ☐	
	L Miss Fun / Late ☐	L Miss Helpful / Tidy ☐
	L Miss Busy / Brainy ☐	L Miss Star / Fun ☐

Please Tick Appropriate Box

may occasionally wish to advise you of other Mr Men gifts.
ou would rather we didn't please tick this box ☐

ENTRANCE FEE SAUSAGES

250 mm

MR. GREEDY

Collect six of these tokens
You will find one inside every
Mr Men and Little Miss book
which has this special offer.

1
TOKEN

Offer open to residents of UK, Channel Isles and Ireland only

Join the
MR.MEN & little miss
Club

Treat your child to membership of the popular Mr Men & Little Miss Club and see their delight when they receive a personal letter from Mr Happy and Little Miss Giggles, a club badge with their name on, and a superb Welcome Pack. And imagine how thrilled they'll be to receive a birthday card and Christmas card from the Mr Men and Little Misses!

Take a look at all of the great things in the Welcome Pack,

every one of them of superb quality (see box right). If it were on sale in the shops, the Pack alone would cost around £12.00. But a year's membership, including all of the other Club benefits, costs just £8.99 (plus 70p postage) with a 14 day money-back guarantee if you're not delighted.

To enrol your child please send your name, address and telephone number together with your child's full name, date of birth and address (including postcode) and a cheque or postal order for £9.69 (payable to Mr Men & Little Miss Club) to: Mr Happy, Happyland (Dept. WI), PO Box 142, Horsham RH13 5FJ. Or call 01403 242727 to pay by credit card.

Please note: Welcome Pack contents may change from time to time. All communications (except the Welcome Pack) will be via parents/guardians. After 30/6/97 please call to check that the price is still valid. Allow 28 days for delivery. Promoter: Robell Media Promotions Limited, registered in England no. 2852153. Your details will be held on computer and may from time to time be made available to reputable companies who we feel have offers of interest to you - please inform us if you do not wish to receive such offers.

The Welcome Pack

✓ Membership card

✓ Personalized badge

✓ Club members' cassette with Mr Men stories and songs

✓ Copy of Mr Men magazine

✓ Mr Men sticker book

✓ Tiny Mr Men flock figure

✓ Mr Men notebook

✓ Mr Men bendy pen

✓ Mr Men eraser

✓ Mr Men book mark

✓ Mr Men key ring

Plus:

✓ Birthday card

✓ Christmas card

✓ Exclusive offers

✓ Easy way to order Mr Men & Little Miss merchandise

All for just £8·99! (plus 70p postage)

MORE SPECIAL OFFERS
FOR MR MEN AND LITTLE MISS READERS

In every Mr Men and Little Miss book like this one, and now in the Mr Men sticker and activity books, you will find a special token. Collect six tokens and we will send you a gift of your choice.

Choose either a Mr Men or Little Miss poster, or a Mr Men or Little Miss **double sided** full colour bedroom door hanger.

Return this page with six tokens per gift required to
Marketing Dept., MM / LM Gifts, World International Ltd., Deanway Technology Centre, Wilmslow Road, Handforth, Cheshire SK9 3FB

|— 100 mm —|

our name:_____ Age: _____

ddress: _____

_____

_____Postcode: _____

arent / Guardian Name (Please Print) _____

ase tape a 20p coin to your request to cover part post and package cost

nclose six tokens per gift, please send me:-

sters:-   Mr Men Poster ☐   Little Miss Poster ☐

or Hangers -   Mr Nosey / Muddle ☐   Mr Greedy / Lazy ☐
            Mr Tickle / Grumpy ☐   Mr Slow / Quiet ☐
            Mr Messy / Noisy ☐
            L Miss Fun / Late ☐   L Miss Helpful / Tidy ☐
            L Miss Busy / Brainy ☐   L Miss Star / Fun ☐

Please Tick Appropriate Box

may occasionally wish to advise you of other Mr Men gifts.
ou would rather we didn't please tick this box ☐

ENTRANCE FEE
SAUSAGES

250 mm

MR. GREEDY

Collect six of these tokens
You will find one inside every
Mr Men and Little Miss book
which has this special offer.

1
TOKEN

Offer open to residents of UK, Channel Isles and Ireland only

Join the
MR.MEN & little miss
Club

Treat your child to membership of the popular Mr Men & Little Miss Club and see their delight when they receive a personal letter from Mr Happy and Little Miss Giggles, a club badge with their name on, and a superb Welcome Pack. And imagine how thrilled they be to receive a birthday card and Christmas card from the Mr Men and Little Misses!

Take a look at all of the great things in the Welcome Pack,

every one of them of superb quality (see box right). If it were on sale in the shops, the Pack alone would cost around £12.00. But a year's membership, including all of the other Club benefits, costs just £8.99 (plus 70p postage) with a 14 day money-back guarantee if you're not delighted.

To enrol your child please send your name, address and telephone number together with your child's full name, date of birth and address (including postcode) and a cheque or postal order for £9.69 (payable to Mr Men & Little Miss Club) to: Mr Happy, Happyland (Dept. WI), PO Box 142, Horsham RH13 5FJ. Or call 01403 242727 to pay by credit card.

The Welcome Pack

✓ Membership card
✓ Personalized badge
✓ Club members' cassette with Mr Men stories and songs
✓ Copy of Mr Men magazine
✓ Mr Men sticker book
✓ Tiny Mr Men flock figure
✓ Mr Men notebook
✓ Mr Men bendy pen
✓ Mr Men eraser
✓ Mr Men book mark
✓ Mr Men key ring

Plus:

✓ Birthday card
✓ Christmas card
✓ Exclusive offers
✓ Easy way to order Mr Men & Little Miss merchandise

All for just £8.99! (plus 70p postage)